D0292009

This Ladybird Book belongs to:

_____

_____

_____

_____

All children have a great ambition … to read by themselves.

Through traditional and popular stories, each title in the **Read It Yourself** series introduces children to the most commonly used words in the English language (*Key Words*), plus additional words necessary to tell the story.

The additional words appearing in this book are listed below.

town, Hamelin, rats, people, rid, mayor, strange, pied, piper, tune, running, fat, thin, different, mountain, lame, paid, played, liked, kept, playing, jumped, drowned, opened, closed

Ladybird books are widely available, but in case of difficulty may be ordered by post or telephone from:

Ladybird Books – Cash Sales Department
Littlegate Road Paignton Devon TQ3 3BE
Telephone 0803 554761

A catalogue record for this book is available
from the British Library

Published by Ladybird Books Ltd Loughborough Leicestershire UK
Ladybird Books Inc Auburn Maine 04210 USA

The Pied Piper of Hamelin

by Fran Hunia

adapted for easy reading from the traditional tale

illustrated by Brian Price Thomas

This was the town of Hamelin.
It was a nice town
but for one thing.

Rats!
Big rats and little rats.
Rats in the shops
and rats in the houses.

There were rats
everywhere!

The people of Hamelin
wanted to get rid of the rats.

One man said,
"What can we do? There are
rats everywhere."

The people said,
"We will go and see the mayor.
He will help us."

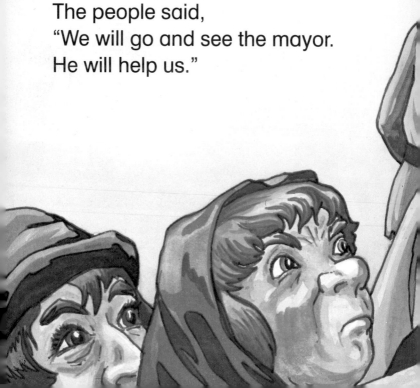

The people went to see
the mayor.

"Please get rid of the rats,"
they said.

The mayor said,
"I don't like the rats.
But what can I do?
I can't make the rats
go away."

"You will have to get rid of the rats, or we will not have you for mayor," said the people.

Then they went home.

A strange man
came to see the mayor.
The strange man
was the pied piper.

The pied piper said
to the mayor,
"Will you give me some money
if I get rid of the rats?"

The mayor said, "Yes,
I will give you all the money
you want if you can make
the rats go away."

The pied piper was pleased.

He played a tune.
A rat came running after him.
Then two rats came.

The pied piper played on.
Soon all the rats in town
were running after
the pied piper.

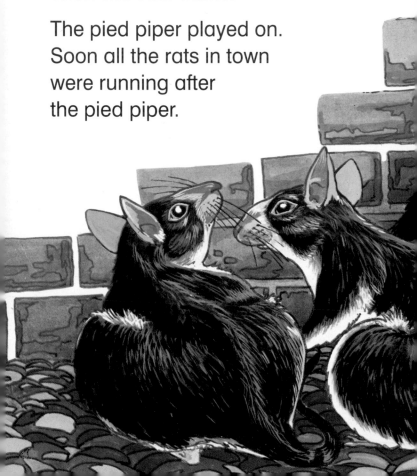

Big rats and little rats,
fat rats and thin rats.
They all liked the tune
that the pied piper
was playing.

They all came running
after him.

The pied piper came
to some water. He kept on playing
his tune.

All the rats jumped into the water
and drowned.

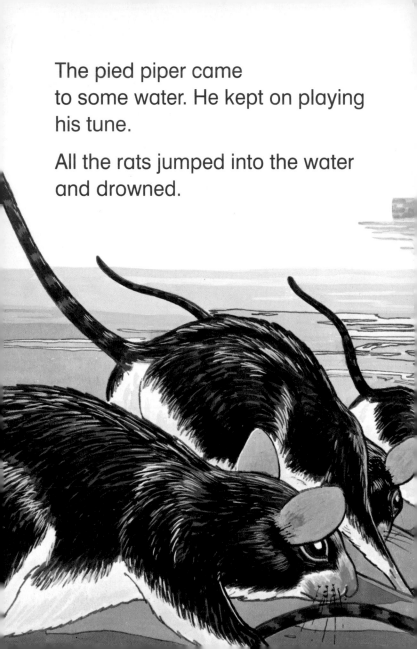

The pied piper said to the mayor,
"The rats have gone.
 Please give me my money."

"No," said the mayor. "I want to
keep the money. The rats have gone
and you can go too. We don't want
you here."

"Give me the money, please,"
said the pied piper.
"Or I will play a different tune!"

"Play away, then," said the mayor.
"You are no danger to me,
and I will not give you
the money you want."

The pied piper played
a different tune.

All the children came
to look at the pied piper.
They liked the tune he was playing
and they all ran after him.

Boys and girls, big ones
and little ones, they all
came running.

The pied piper came
to the water,
but the children didn't
jump in.

The pied piper kept on playing
the tune that the children liked.
He went into the mountain,
and the children went in
after him.

There were trees and flowers
in the mountain.

The pied piper went on
and the children ran after him.
They came to a mountain,
but they didn't stop.

The mountain opened up.

One boy was lame,
and could not keep up
with the pied piper.
He wanted to go in,
but the mountain closed up.

The boy had to go home.
He had no one to play with.
All the children were
in the mountain.

The mayor looked everywhere
for the pied piper
and the children,
but it was no good.
They had gone.

He should have paid
the pied piper the money.

LADYBIRD
READING SCHEMES

Read It Yourself links with all Ladybird reading schemes and can be used with any other method of learning to read.

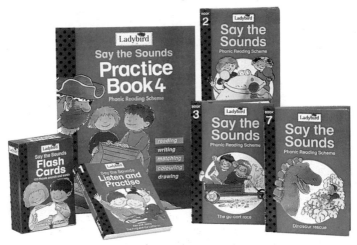

Say the Sounds

Ladybird's **Say the Sounds** graded reading scheme is a *phonics* scheme. It teaches children the sounds of individual letters and letter combinations, enabling them to tackle new words by building them up as a blend of smaller units.

There are 8 titles in this scheme:

1 **Rocket to the jungle**
2 **Frog and the lollipops**
3 **The go-cart race**
4 **Pirate's treasure**
5 **Humpty Dumpty and the robots**
6 **Flying saucer**
7 **Dinosaur rescue**
8 **The accident**

Support material available: Practice Books, Double Cassette pack, Flash Cards